Para Amparo
G. G.

Thank you, Maya!
R. A.

First published in 2011 by
Gullane Children's Books

185 Fleet Street, London, EC4A 2HS
www.gullanebooks.com

2   4   6   8   10   9   7   5   3   1

Text © Greg Gormley 2011
Illustrations © Roberta Angaramo 2011

A CIP record for this title is available from the British Library.

ISBN-978-1-86233-800-5

Printed and bound in China

Dog in Boots

Greg Gormley • Roberta Angaramo

GULLANE
CHILDREN'S BOOKS

Dog was reading a brilliant book, all about a cat
who wore a pair of truly magnificent boots.

When he finished reading, Dog put down his book
and had a little think.

Then he went to the local shoe shop.

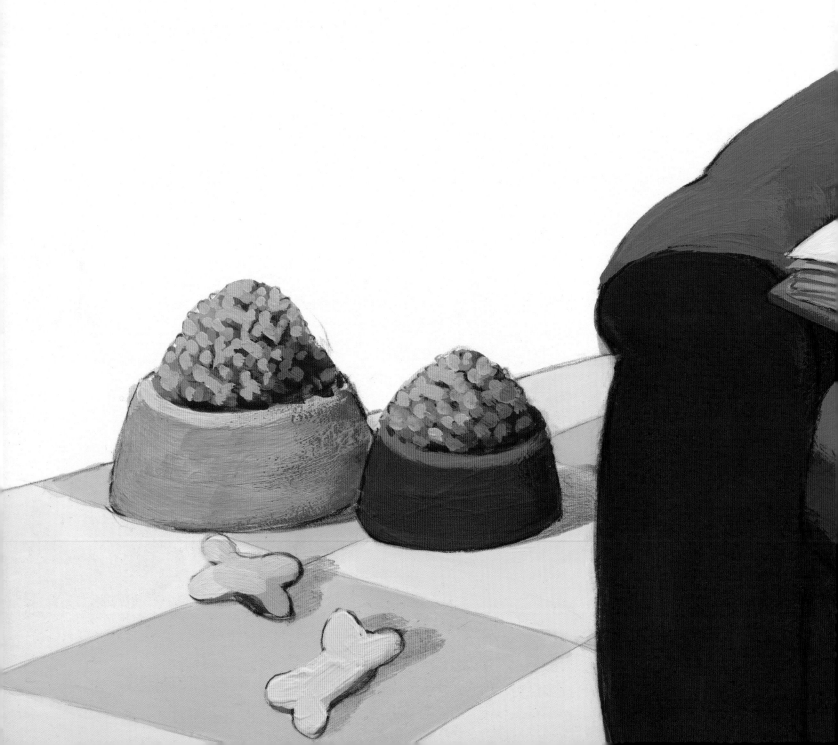

"Have you got any footwear as splendid as this?"
he said, showing the book to the shopkeeper.
"I believe I have," said the shopkeeper, and brought out four
just as splendid boots, one for each of Dog's paws.
"Bow WOW!" said Dog. "I'll take them."

Dog was so pleased that he went straight home . . .

to dig up his very best bone.

But the new boots were not at all splendid or magnificent for digging.
And they got so muddy that they looked quite awful.

So Dog took them back to the shop.

"Have you got some that are better for digging?" he asked.
"I have just the thing," said the shopkeeper.
"These **welly boots** are perfect in mud –
it simply washes right off."

The welly boots were wonderful for digging . . .

but when Dog went for a swim in the pond, they **filled up with water** and he sank with a

PLOP!

Dog took them back to the shop.

"Have you got some that are better for swimming?" he asked.
"The best thing for swimming," the shopkeeper said, "is
flippers."

The flippers were fantastic
for swimming . . .

but when Dog tried to scratch . . .

they **flip-flap-flopped** around his head . . .

in a very unsatisfying way.

Dog took them back to the shop.

"Have you got some that are better for scratching?" he said.
"I'm glad you asked," said the shopkeeper. "With these
high heels you can scratch – and look
rather fashionable at the same time."

For scratching behind Dog's ears,
the high heels were simply divine . . .

unfortunately they were dreadful to run in –
he went flying head over high heels!

Dog took them back to the shop.

"Have you got some that go a bit faster?" he asked.
"Oh yes," said the shopkeeper. "If you want to go super-fast,
try **skis.** They go very fast indeed—"
"I'll take them!" said Dog.

And he was gone before the shopkeeper could say

". . . but only on snow!"

Without any snow, Dog's skis didn't move at all.

He couldn't run

or scratch

or swim

or dig.

On his way back to the shop, Dog had another little think . . .

"OK," he said to the shopkeeper. "I want something that's good
for digging and swimming and scratching and running.
Oh, nice and furry too. Do you have anything like that?"

"No," said the shopkeeper, "but YOU do.
They're called . . .

"PAWS!"

"Perfect!" said Dog.

Dog was so pleased with his nice, furry, practical paws,
that he scratched all the fleas from his coat . . .

ran after his tail . . .

swam round and round the Queen's lake,
until she told him to clear off . . .

and dug a big hole to rebury his very best bone.

Finally Dog went home and
picked out another brilliant book to read.

This time it was about a girl,
who didn't wear any rubbish boots, but did wear . . .

a lovely red hood!

"Mmmm . . ." thought Dog.

Little Red Riding Hood